Mr. Putter and Tabby
Row the Boat

CYNTHIA RYLANT

Mr. Putter and Tabby Row the Boat

Illustrated by

ARTHUR HOWARD

Harcourt Brace & Company

San Diego   New York   London

For Dav, who rowed the boat
—*C. R.*

For Rebecca Tess Howard
—*A. H.*

Text copyright © 1997 by Cynthia Rylant
Illustrations copyright © 1997 by Arthur Howard

Requests for permission to make
copies of any part of the work should be mailed to:
Permissions Department, Harcourt Brace & Company,
6277 Sea Harbor Drive,
Orlando, Florida 32887-6777.

Library of Congress Cataloging-in-Publication Data
Rylant, Cynthia.
Mr. Putter and Tabby row the boat/Cynthia Rylant;
illustrated by Arthur Howard.—1st ed.
p. cm.
Summary: On a hot summer day, Mr. Putter, his cat, Tabby, their neighbor
Mrs. Teaberry and her dog, Zeke, go for a picnic and a rowboat ride.
ISBN 0-15-256257-5
ISBN 0-15-201059-9 (pbk.)
[1. Heat—Fiction. 2. Pets—Fiction. 3. Picnicking—Fiction.]
I. Howard, Arthur, ill. II. Title.
PZ7.R982Mu 1997
[E]—dc20   93-41832

Printed in Singapore

First edition
A C E F D B
A C E F D B (pbk.)

1
Sweaty

It was summer
and the weather was very hot.
Mr. Putter and his fine cat, Tabby,
lay around all day and sweated.

They sweated on the front porch.

They sweated in the kitchen.

They sweated under the oak tree.

They even tried the basement,
but they sweated there, too.

"We're too old to sweat like this,"
Mr. Putter told Tabby.
"We shouldn't have any sweat left in us."
But they did,
and they were miserable.

Then Mr. Putter had an idea.
"Let's go to the big pond,"
he said to Tabby.
"We'll take Mrs. Teaberry and Zeke."
Their neighbors—Mrs. Teaberry and
her good dog, Zeke—were sweaty, too.

Mr. Putter was sure of it
because he had just seen Mrs. Teaberry
dump a bowl of water on Zeke's head.

He went to Mrs. Teaberry and
told her his idea.

She thought a trip to the pond
was a wonderful idea.
She said that she would
make tomato sandwiches.

She would fix a kiwi salad.

She would fill a jug
with apple tea.

Mr. Putter smiled.

He liked Mrs. Teaberry's funny food.

He went home to get Tabby ready.

They were going to the big pond.

2

The Big Pond

The big pond was not far away,
so Mr. Putter and Tabby
and Mrs. Teaberry and Zeke walked.

It was a hot walk.

It was a sweaty walk.

It was a slow walk.

But it got exciting.

Mrs. Teaberry was wearing
a big, wide hat covered with
fake red grapes.
A blue jay kept trying
to steal the grapes.
He swooped down and grabbed
Mrs. Teaberry's hat from her head.

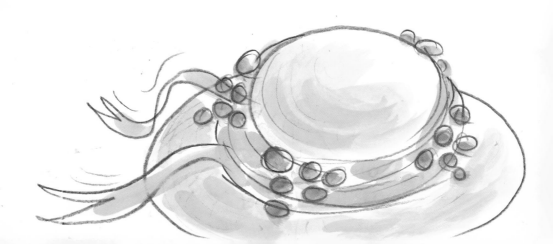

"Shoo!" said Mrs. Teaberry.
"Scat!" said Mr. Putter.
Tabby and Zeke were
too hot to do anything.

Mr. Putter and Mrs. Teaberry
couldn't help laughing at the silly bird.

Finally Mrs. Teaberry gave it
some kiwi salad and it flew away.

When they got to the big pond,
there was a woman there
renting rowboats.
Two dollars for two hours,
she told them.
Mr. Putter and Mrs. Teaberry
looked at each other.
"What a deal!" they said.

They loaded up Tabby
and Zeke
and lunch
and rowed away.

Tabby curled up under
one of the seats.
Zeke tried to drink
out of the pond.
And Mr. Putter and Mrs. Teaberry
headed for a good shady place.

3
Tall Tales

Mr. Putter spotted a clump
of pine trees that made
a good shady place.

When they reached the place,
Mrs. Teaberry took off her hat.

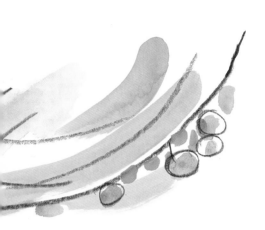

Many of her fake red grapes
were missing.
But she didn't mind.
She filled the hat with water
and dumped it on Zeke's head.
Zeke loved it.

Tabby came out from under her seat.
She batted at a water bug
on the pond.

Her tail twitched.
Her teeth clicked.

She forgot all about being hot.
She just wanted that bug.

Mr. Putter and Mrs. Teaberry
took off their shoes
and put their feet in the water.
They filled their cups with apple tea.
They chewed their tomato sandwiches.
And they finished what was left
of their kiwi salad.

They told each other
tall tales from their lives.
Mr. Putter told about the time
he won the county worm race.
He said his worm's name was Jack.

Mrs. Teaberry told about the time
she won three hundred dollars.
She said she spent it all
on nail polish.

They laughed and laughed
at each other's stories.

Zeke drank the pond,
Tabby batted the bug,
and everyone was happy.

4

Much Better

When it was time to row the boat back,
Mr. Putter and Tabby weren't
sweating anymore.
Mrs. Teaberry and Zeke were
cool as cucumbers.
The trip had been a success.

They left the rowboat with the
rowboat woman and began
the walk home.
It was a hot walk.
It was a sweaty walk.
It was a slow walk.

When they got home, they were
all as hot as when they left.
No one knew what to do.

Then Mrs. Teaberry filled up her hat . . .

. . . and dumped water

on everybody's head.

Even her own.

And they all felt much better.

The illustrations in this book were done in pencil, watercolor,
gouache, and Sennelier pastels on 90-pound vellum paper.
The display type was set in Artcraft and the
text type was set in Berkeley Old Style Book.
Color separations were made by United Graphic Pte Ltd., Singapore.
Printed and bound by Tien Wah Press, Singapore
This book was printed on Nymolla Matte Art paper.
Production supervision by Stanley Redfern and Pascha Gerlinger
Designed by Arthur Howard and Carolyn Stafford